MARV

AND THE
KILLER
PLANTS

DEAR READER,

Recently, I moved to a home with a garden. It's not a very big garden—I can walk from one end to the other in three or four big steps—but it's mine now, so I have to look after it.

When I came here, the garden was overgrown with weeds and the earth was filled with rocks, so I thought it would be a cool project to try and fix it—to turn all of that mess into lush, green grass.

Was it hard? Yes. I had to spend hours clearing the weeds and rocks, then I had to plant new grass seeds, and after all of that, I had to water the grass twice a day to get it to grow.

However, transforming the garden was one of the best things I've done all year. I think that's because gardening gives you a very visual reminder of something essential. When you work really hard at something, magical things can happen. The world itself can change around you. It may not happen all at once, but it does happen day by day, minute by minute, step by step. You only have to look. A weedy, rocky garden can become beautiful.

Alex

That's me!

For my cats Akira and Simone – A.F-K

For SUPER YOU, the completely marvellous reader – P.B

OXFORD
UNIVERSITY PRESS

Great Clarendon Street, Oxford OX2 6DP
Oxford University Press is a department of the University of Oxford.
It furthers the University's objective of excellence in research, scholarship,
and education by publishing worldwide. Oxford is a registered trade mark
of Oxford University Press in the UK and in certain other countries

British Library Cataloguing in Publication Data

Data available

ISBN: 978-0-19-278050-8

1 3 5 7 9 10 8 6 4 2

Printed in China

Paper used in the production of this book is a natural,
recyclable product made from wood grown in sustainable forests.
The manufacturing process conforms to the environmental
regulations of the country of origin.

MARV

AND THE
KILLER PLANTS

WRITTEN BY
ALEX FALASE-KOYA

PICTURES BY
PAULA BOWLES

OXFORD
UNIVERSITY PRESS

CHAPTER 1

Marvin ducked and weaved along the overgrown track, dodging the giant palm leaves.

'Come on, Grandad!' Marvin called, as he hurried deeper into the botanical gardens.

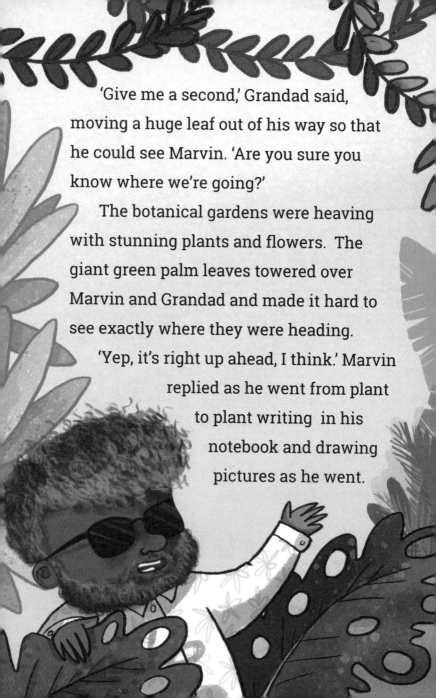

'Give me a second,' Grandad said, moving a huge leaf out of his way so that he could see Marvin. 'Are you sure you know where we're going?'

The botanical gardens were heaving with stunning plants and flowers. The giant green palm leaves towered over Marvin and Grandad and made it hard to see exactly where they were heading.

'Yep, it's right up ahead, I think.' Marvin replied as he went from plant to plant writing in his notebook and drawing pictures as he went.

Marvin's school were having a competition to design a brand-new garden for the school grounds, and Marvin was determined to win. He'd persuaded Grandad to take him to the botanical gardens to get some ideas for his school garden design. It was a big deal because the forest school were going to use the garden, as well as the local community. All kinds of special events would be taking place there. Marvin closed his eyes for a moment, practically vibrating with excitement. He could imagine it now; his garden design winning and becoming reality. It would be

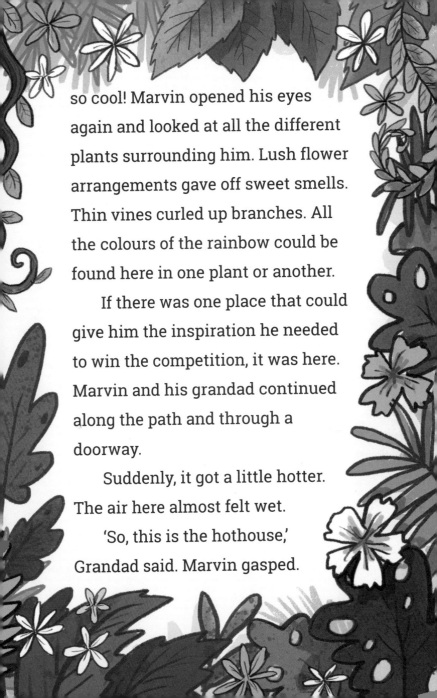

so cool! Marvin opened his eyes again and looked at all the different plants surrounding him. Lush flower arrangements gave off sweet smells. Thin vines curled up branches. All the colours of the rainbow could be found here in one plant or another.

If there was one place that could give him the inspiration he needed to win the competition, it was here. Marvin and his grandad continued along the path and through a doorway.

Suddenly, it got a little hotter. The air here almost felt wet.

'So, this is the hothouse,' Grandad said. Marvin gasped.

Marvin had read about the different areas within the botanical gardens, and he was looking forward to visiting the hothouse most of all. It was full of tropical plants that ordinarily only grew in hot places around the world.

Big Venus flytraps with large yawning mouths stood frighteningly still, as though waiting to pounce on their next meal. Huge ferns with long flapping leaves swayed gently from side to side. Thick green vines had woven themselves across the floor reaching every corner of the hothouse.

It was amazing. Marvin had never seen plants like this before. His favourites were the insect-eating Venus flytraps. It would be OK, Marvin thought, if he just gave the Venus flytrap a little test. Marvin picked up a small piece of grass from the floor and reached out towards one of the Venus flytraps. The piece of grass tickled the inside of the flytrap's mouth, and then in a couple of seconds, it happened.

'Woah!' Marvin said, as the mouth of the Venus flytrap slowly closed around the grass.

Marvin sketched the Venus flytrap as best he could.

'Marvin, I'm going to head outside
and find a good spot for our picnic. Don't
get into any trouble,' Grandad said.

'Yes, Grandad.'

All of a sudden, a high-pitched beeping came from Marvin's backpack. He froze and looked around carefully, making sure that no one else was in the hothouse with him. Then when he was absolutely sure that he was alone, Marvin put his backpack on the ground and opened it up. A shiny, silvery metal head poked out of the top.

It was Pixel, Marvin's robot sidekick. Sure, Marvin looked like an ordinary boy, but he had a secret. He was also Marv! A superhero with a super-suit powered by kindness and imagination. Pixel was his trusty robot companion, and he took her and his super-suit with him everywhere, just in case.

Pixel's round eyes scanned over the plants in the room.

'Wouldn't it be cool, Pixel, if our school garden had a version of this hothouse with Venus flytraps in it?!' Marvin said, waving his arms with excitement.

'I'm sensing danger! What if Venus flytraps like the taste of robot?' Pixel replied.

'I'm sure they don't,' Marvin said, but Pixel still looked worried.

She reached out to touch one of the Venus flytraps and then seemed to change her mind, whipping her robot arm back.

'There's a one hundred per cent chance that these plants are untrustworthy.'

'How'd you come up with that number?' Marvin said. She was normally pretty good at calculating things (she was a robot after all) but how could she be so sure?

'I just have a bad feeling,' Pixel said, crossing her long, spindly, robot arms.

'Come on Pixel. These plants aren't harmful to humans . . . or robots! And if there ever was a problem . . .' Marvin reached past Pixel into his backpack and

pulled out the sleeve of his blue
super-suit. 'Marv and Pixel will be on
hand to save the day. With the two of us
together there's no problem we can't solve.'

'OK, Marvin. I guess you are right.'
Pixel finally stopped frowning. She
reached up and gave Marvin a high five,
beeping excitedly. 'But if you're wrong you
owe me cookies!'

Marvin laughed.

'All right. I'll see you later, Pixel. I should go find Grandad,' Marvin said.

Pixel got back into the backpack and Marvin put it on, heading out of the hothouse to meet his grandad.

Marvin sat with a pencil in one hand and a sandwich in the other. Even during lunch, he was still perfecting his school garden design. He was getting close now, only a little bit more and then it would be per—

'Hey Marvin!' a familiar voice broke him out of his creative bubble. He looked up to see one of his friends from class, Eva, walking towards him. Her mum and her sister trailed behind.

'Eva, what a surprise! Here, have a seat,' said Grandad, getting up off the bench. 'I'm going to go say hello to your mum.'

'You came to the botanical gardens too!' Eva said. 'Research, right? For the school garden project?'

Marvin frowned, he couldn't remember mentioning his plan to come to the botanical gardens to Eva.

'Yeah, that's why I'm here, but why are you here?' he asked.

Eva held up a thick sketchbook.

'I'm doing the same thing,' she replied. 'After all, if you want to make the best design you have to do your research.'

'You want to win the school garden design competition too?'

Eva peered closely at his notebook.

Marvin threw his arms over it, but he was too late—Eva had already seen his design.

'Wow! That's cool, Marvin, I like your hothouse idea,' Eva said.

'I'm still working on it, I'm not really ready to share yet.' Marvin shut his notebook.

'I've got something that's a little similar.' Eva opened up her sketchbook. Marvin's eyes grew wide. She was right, the designs *were* similar. Had Eva been following him around the gardens and copying his ideas?

'Those are actually really good.' Marv felt a knot of worry in his stomach. He'd been so certain that he'd have the best design, but now he wasn't so sure.

'Do you want to look around the gardens together?' Eva asked.

Marvin was about to say 'yes' but stopped himself. He wanted to have fun with Eva, but he didn't know if he trusted her not to copy his ideas.

'No, I have to do more work on my design,' Marvin finally said.

'Sure. I'd love to see it when you're done,' Eva said. 'I'll see you at school.' And with that, she skipped off into the hothouse, with her mum and sister.

When Marvin and Grandad had finished their picnic, they headed home. Marvin kept thinking about his design. Was it just coincidence that his and Eva's designs were so similar?

Next week at school, Marvin handed in his garden design. He'd worked so hard on it that he was sure it would win.

Over the next few days' excitement grew until the day the winner was to be announced. Marvin and his best friend Joe were sat together in the crowded assembly hall. Marvin shivered; his chest was pounding with anticipation.

'Do you think I can win?' he asked Joe.

'Yeah, definitely, your design was so cool,' Joe said without even hesitating. Marvin's heart settled. He was glad he had Joe on his side. It was good that someone else thought he could win.

The excited whispers in the hall hushed as the headteacher took to the stage.

She called for quiet.

'And the winner of the school garden competition is . . . drum roll, please . . .' All the kids in the hall drummed their hands against the floor, and then the headteacher said it. 'Eva Kowalski!'

Marvin's heart sank. He glanced around the room until he found Eva. She was beaming. Marvin frowned. How had he lost? Marvin had made the trip to the botanical gardens especially and had spent hours researching and making notes.

This was the hardest he had ever worked at school on anything, and he had still lost. Marvin remembered how interested Eva had been in his design when they met at the botanical gardens. Marvin couldn't help but wonder—what if he lost because Eva cheated and copied his design?

CHAPTER 2

Marvin thought about Eva cheating all day. In fact, he was still thinking about it at dinner when he got home.

'What's on your mind, little one?' Grandad asked.

'Nothing.' Marvin sighed. 'Well, maybe not nothing.' Grandad listened carefully as Marvin told him all about the competition at school and how Eva had won.

'So, you think Eva might have stolen your design?' Grandad asked.

'Yes, you see it too! Right?' Marvin
said. But for some reason, Grandad didn't
seem annoyed at what Eva had done.

'What Eva did was awful, right?'
Marvin said slowly, waiting for Grandad
to confirm.

Grandad simply smiled and shrugged.

'Let me tell you a story.' Grandad said. 'When I was around your age there was a spelling competition at my school. The prizes for the top three places were these really cool certificates saying how smart we were. I wanted to win really,

really badly, so I spent a whole month studying all sorts of words.'

'And you won?' Marvin blurted out.

Grandad cackled to himself.

'No, I actually came fourth,' he said.

'You just missed getting one of those certificates. That must have been awful.'

'Yep! At first, I was so disappointed because I had put in all that hard work and got nothing in return. But when I thought about it, I realized that all the hard work I put in meant that I had a whole bunch of new spellings memorized. I mean, I can still spell "antihistamine" without any trouble, to this day!' Grandad pulled down his sunglasses and gave Marvin a wink.

'Anti what?' Marvin raised his eyebrows.

'All I'm trying to say is that you'll still get to enjoy the amazing garden, right? And you also learnt a lot about gardens and plants when you were designing your own competition entry. That's pretty great, isn't it?' Grandad reached over and rested a hand on Marvin's shoulder.

'Yeah, I guess so,' Marvin said with a shrug. Deep down, he knew that Grandad was right, but even so, something inside him still felt like it was unfair.

The next day, there was a great rumble in the school playground. A lorry filled with soil and a couple of diggers were working on the garden already. It was being built just to the left of the main school building.

'This is the best!' Joe cried out.

'Is it really?' Marvin sighed.

'Yeah, because Eva won, our whole class gets to spend the day helping to plant flowers and trees. No lessons for us!' Joe whooped.

'Hey, guys!' Eva said, walking over with several pots full of beautiful flowers in her arms. 'This is all so exciting, isn't it?!'

'Yeah!' Joe said.

'I guess so,' Marvin added.

Eva handed some of the flower pots to Marvin and Joe.

'It would be cool if you could help us plant these,' she said.

'Of course we will. Just tell us where,' Joe replied.

'Well, the grown-ups are still deciding exactly how it's all going to work but let me show you my design.' Eva put the rest of the flowers on the ground and then reached into her backpack for her design.

Marvin perked up. He wanted to get a closer look at the design that beat his own.

A hothouse. Eva's design had a hothouse too! In fact, it sort of looked like the one Marvin had in *his* design. And that wasn't the only thing—there were lots of other elements that looked really similar too.

34

Marvin's fists clenched tight and suddenly his face felt really hot. Before he could stop himself he shouted at Eva.

'You stole my design, didn't you?!'

'W-what are you talking about?' Eva took an unsteady step back.

'Yeah, Marvin, are you sure about this?' Joe tried to put a hand on Marvin's shoulder, but he shrugged Joe's hand away.

'My design had a hothouse, just like this one! You cheated! You stole my design!' Marvin furiously prodded at Eva's design as he yelled.

'I'm not a cheater!' Eva blushed hard and then stormed away.

Marvin huffed and then turned to Joe, expecting to see sympathy in his eyes, but it wasn't there.

'Are you sure that Eva stole your design? I don't think she would have done something like that,' Joe said.

'Then how did she have exactly the

same hothouse idea as me?' Marvin
threw up his hands in frustration.

'Well, how did you get the hothouse
idea in the first place?' Joe asked.

'I visited one at the botanical
gardens,' Marvin said.

'Wait, Eva told me that she went
there too.' Joe raised his eyebrows.

'Yeah, so?'

'What if she just had the same inspiration as you?' Joe shrugged.

'Yes! She only went to the hothouse because she saw it on my design,' Marvin said.

Joe didn't reply this time, and just looked a bit awkward. Marvin couldn't believe Joe. He was supposed to be his best friend, but it was clear he was on Eva's side. 'You know what I think? I want to be by myself for a bit.' Before Joe could say anything else, Marvin stomped off.

Marvin didn't even really know where he was going at first, he just wanted to get away. And then he had an idea.

There was a great hiding place that Marvin sometimes used when they all played hide and seek. It was behind a bin right in the corner of the bottom playing field. No one would be able to see him over there.

Marvin was crouched behind the bin feeling sorry for himself when a high-pitched beeping sound filled the air. Marvin glanced down at his backpack just in time to see Pixel pop her head out of it.

'By my calculations, there's a ninety-nine per cent chance that the garden will be finished quicker with our help.'

'I don't think I want to go back. I can just stay here behind the bin. No one will notice that I'm missing. No one cares.'

'There's a one hundred per cent chance that what you just said is incorrect.'

'You're just trying to be nice, but you can't convince me. I'm not moving. I even have my lunchbox with me so there's no reason to move for the rest of the day,' Marvin said.

Marvin was cross but he couldn't escape a niggling feeling inside. What if Eva, Joe, and Grandad had a point? Eva and Joe could be wrong, because they both liked pineapple on pizza, and that was the most wrong thing ever, and surely Joe was just sticking up for Eva because they were friends. But Grandad didn't seem to think that Eva cheated either. And Grandad was almost always right.

Just then, a huge crashing sound came from the other side of the playground, from where the new garden was going to be. At first, Marvin thought that maybe it was a problem with one of the diggers but then a voice cried out.

'Someone help! We need a superhero. Where's Marv when you need him?'

Pixel beeped loudly.

'Eating lunch behind a bin will have to wait. It's time to be a hero!' she said.

CHAPTER 3

Marvin sighed as he got to his feet. He didn't really feel like being a superhero right now, but he couldn't ignore those screams and shouts. He had to put his feelings to one side. Marvin quickly got his super-suit out of his backpack and put it on. He was no longer Marvin—he was now Marv!

'Supervillain detected. Supervillain detected!' Pixel bleated as they made their way back to the garden.

'Yes Pixel, I can hear you,' Marv said as he ran—Pixel hovering beside him.

'Supervillain det—' Pixel didn't finish. Her head spun round and round in a panic. Marv gasped when he saw it too.

The unfinished school garden had been transformed into a thick jungle. Huge creeping vines slithered out in all directions, growing longer by the second. Marv knew that if he didn't do something, the jungle might take over the whole school, and maybe even the whole town!

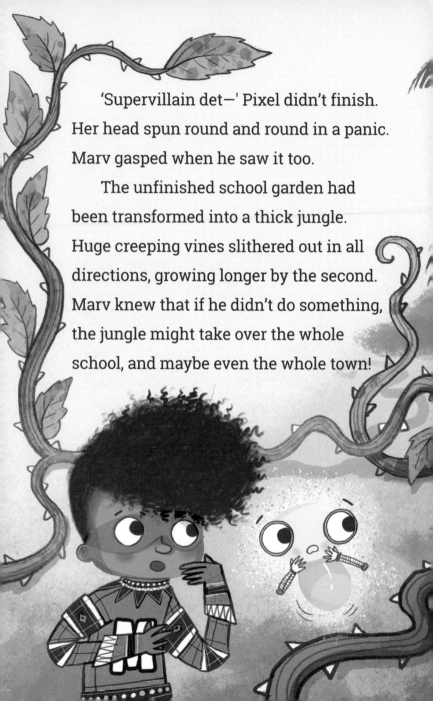

All around Marv his classmates were shouting for help. They were all tangled up in the vines! Some of them hung upside down, while others were being pulled along by the vines.

Even the diggers
were wrapped up by
hundreds of vines. They
hung from a giant tree
like Christmas baubles.

'Who did this?' Marv cried.

"Tis I! Violet Vine, sweet by name and spiky by nature!' Marv looked up to where the voice was coming from. A girl around his age was sitting on top of a thick vine.

It slithered across the garden floor like a giant snake, bringing the girl closer. She had a green super-suit of her own with a small satchel strapped across her chest.

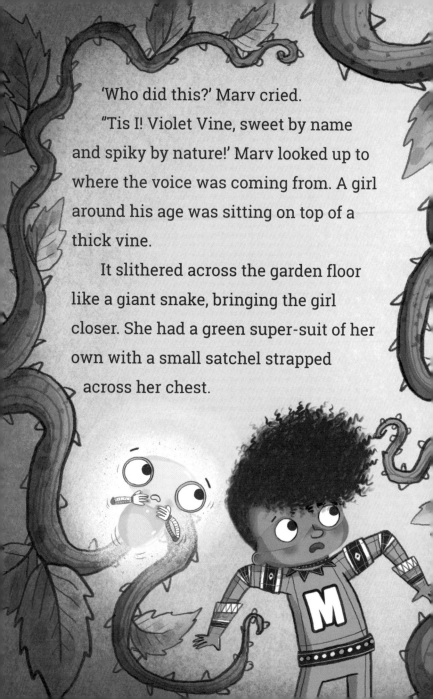

'Why are you doing this?' Marv said.

'Because she's a supervillain', remember, *supervillain detected*,' Pixel whispered.

'I know, just more specifically,' Marv whispered back.

Violet Vine cleared her throat, making sure their attention was on her before she began to speak.

'I heard about a new garden being designed at this pathetic little school,' she said.

'What's wrong with that?' Marv shrugged.

'The design for this garden is fine. If being REALLY BORING is your thing. So I thought I'd come and make a few adjustments. And then I thought, if I'm improving the garden, I might as well transform the whole school too.' Violet Vine cackled.

'But you can't just turn a school into a jungle! And you can't just trap the students!' Marv pointed to his friends still swinging from the vines.

'This place will make a fabulous evil lair for me. And the students?' Violet cackled again. 'They'll make great plant food.'

Violet Vine rummaged around in her satchel and then pulled something out and threw it onto the ground. Suddenly, a giant green stem rocketed up from the earth, and at the very top of it was a large, dark mouth. It was a giant Venus flytrap! It shuffled away on its tentacle-like roots into the undergrowth and out of sight. Violet Vine laughed again, running off in the opposite direction towards the school.

'Get me down from here!' A voice called out from above. Marv looked up to see Joe dangling by his ankle from a branch on the tree. A vine wrapped around his leg was all that held him in place.

The branch he was hanging from gave a big creak.

Joe squeaked.

The Venus flytrap and Violet Vine could wait—Marv had to save Joe right now.

He placed a hand over the 'M' on his suit.

'It's super-suit time! Super-suit, please activate super suction cups!' As Marv leapt up onto the tree, suction cups sprouted from the arms and legs of his super-suit, helping him climb up the tree at a rapid pace.

Pixel shot a net out of her chest and held it out under Joe.

'Please don't let me fall,' Joe said.

'I won't,' Marv replied. He glanced down and his belly wobbled a little. He was a long, long way from the ground.

If he was going to help Joe, Marv had to do something about that vine.

Marv reached out and pulled the vine around Joe's leg, but it held fast.

Marv pressed his hand onto the 'M' on his suit and thought really hard, then it came to him!

'Please super-suit, activate finger laser.'

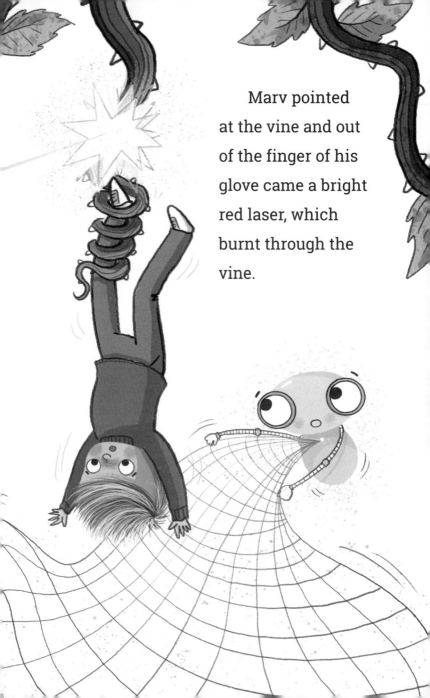

Marv pointed at the vine and out of the finger of his glove came a bright red laser, which burnt through the vine.

Joe cried out as he broke free of the vine and fell into Pixel's net. Pixel slowly lowered Joe from the tree as Marv scurried back down using his suction cups.

'Thanks, Marv,' Joe said as he reached the ground.

Marv appreciated Joe saying thanks, but he had no time to hang around. He had to stop that Venus flytrap!

'Marv! I could really do with your help right now!' Someone's voice called out and they sounded like they were in trouble. Marv followed the sound of the voice into the thick green undergrowth. He knew whoever was calling him needed his help and Marv just hoped he wasn't too late.

CHAPTER 4

Marv spotted the person up ahead. Well, he spotted a bit of them. Their legs were waving frantically from the jaws of the giant Venus flytrap. The rest of them was buried deep into the flytrap's mouth.

'Hang in there, I'm coming!' Marv yelled up at them.

As Marv ran towards the Venus flytrap, vines slithered around his feet trying to trip him up. Pixel found it hard to keep up, as leaves of giant flowers blocked her way, almost trapping her too.

'I can't believe Violet Vine said my design was boring,' the person in the giant Venus flytrap said. The voice sounded familiar.

It was Eva.

Marv hesitated for a second. He was still annoyed with Eva, but deep down he knew she didn't deserve to get eaten by a Venus flytrap—no one did.

Marv leapt onto the stem of the Venus flytrap and used his suction cups again, to pull himself all the way up to Eva. Super strength rushed into the arms of his super-suit. Marv's arms suddenly felt bigger, but at the same time lighter than they ever had before. He jammed his hands into the gigantic flytrap's mouth and then pulled as hard as he could. Marv grunted as he slowly dragged open the jaws of the Venus flytrap before pulling Eva out and carrying her safely back down to the ground.

'Eww, that Venus flytrap needs to brush its teeth!' Eva said, looking a little green, but otherwise unharmed.

The monster plant swung its head down and snapped at Marv and Eva. They both leapt back. Marv had to stop it!

An idea jumped into his head.

Marv grabbed onto one of the nearby vines and then ran in circles around the Venus flytrap. Marv got faster and faster with each completed circle until he was at super-speed. His hair and his super-suit rippled around in the whooshing air. Then Marv skidded to a stop.

'I guess that's a wrap,' Pixel said, pointing up at the giant Venus flytrap now totally wrapped up in Marv's vine.

'Hey—that was a good joke, Pixel!' Marv said.

'I read in my sidekick handbook that witty jokes are essential, so I've been practising at home,' Pixel replied.

The killer plant had been stopped for now, but Marv knew that if Violet Vine could make one giant Venus flytrap, she could make another.

Marv suddenly sneezed and looked down at his hands. They were covered in weird, powdery dust. It looked as though it had come from the vine itself. The powder was ever so slightly green and

glittery. It was definitely weird, but Marv
didn't have time to investigate—he had
to go after Violet Vine!

'Eva, team up with Joe and try and
free the rest of the class,' Marv said.

'What are you going to do, Marv?' Eva
asked.

'I'm going to put a stop to Violet
Vine!'

A trail of vines and large jungle plants went all the way from the school garden to the school building. Marv and Pixel followed it.

Leaves and plants poked out of the classroom windows and almost blocked the entrance completely. School kids were streaming out of the building,

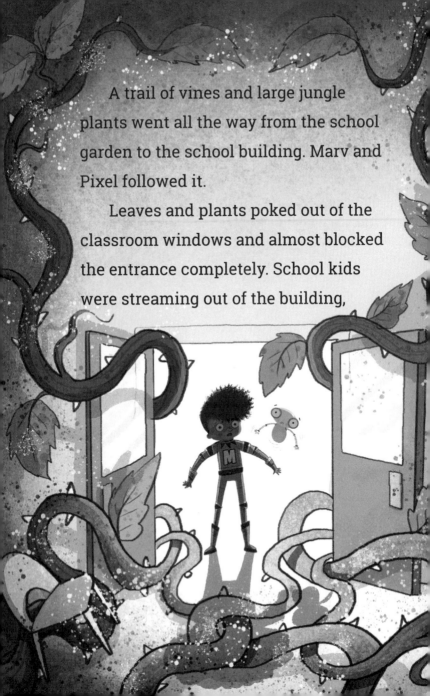

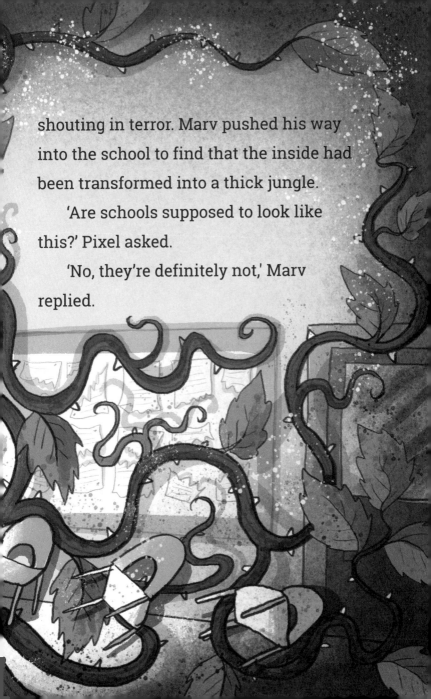

shouting in terror. Marv pushed his way into the school to find that the inside had been transformed into a thick jungle.

'Are schools supposed to look like this?' Pixel asked.

'No, they're definitely not,' Marv replied.

A teacher was poking a vine with a chair, trying to keep it back. The vines had taken over practically all of the school, and they were slowly covering the classrooms. Huge plants and trees lined the hallways and windows. There was hardly any sign that it was once a school at all. Violet Vine had to be stopped!

Just then, a big fern came waddling down the corridor. It was carrying Marv's headteacher!

'Marv, it's . . . great to see you . . .
give you a tour if it wasn't for . . . badly
behaved plants . . . simply not the kind
of behaviour . . . expected at school.' Her
voice was a bit muffled by the plant, but
Marv mostly understood.

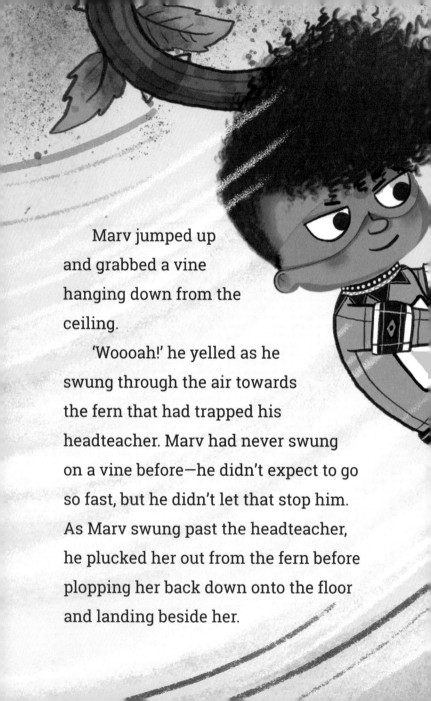

Marv jumped up and grabbed a vine hanging down from the ceiling.

'Woooah!' he yelled as he swung through the air towards the fern that had trapped his headteacher. Marv had never swung on a vine before—he didn't expect to go so fast, but he didn't let that stop him. As Marv swung past the headteacher, he plucked her out from the fern before plopping her back down onto the floor and landing beside her.

'Thank you, Marv, for helping us out.'
The headteacher dusted herself down.
'That dreadful supervillain, Violet Vine,
was heading for the library. You have
to stop her.' Marv nodded and began to
run again, deeper into the jungle school.
As he did, Marv heard his headteacher's
voice echo after him. 'Hurry! The future
of the school is at stake!'

CHAPTER 5

Marv skidded to a stop in the library and almost immediately sneezed. The room was filled with vines—they had knocked over the bookshelves and scattered the books across the floor.

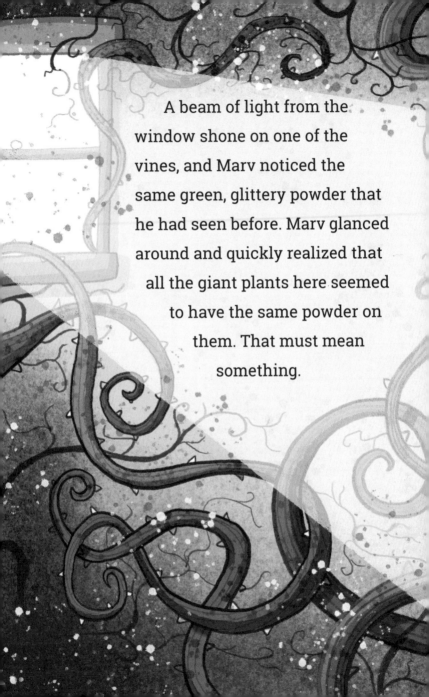

A beam of light from the window shone on one of the vines, and Marv noticed the same green, glittery powder that he had seen before. Marv glanced around and quickly realized that all the giant plants here seemed to have the same powder on them. That must mean something.

'Pixel, can you please scan that powder?' Marv asked. He remembered that the giant Venus flytrap hadn't appeared out of nowhere—Violet Vine had thrown something on the ground first.

Pixel swooped over the vine, brushing her fingers along it to collect the strange dust.

'My diagnostics are detecting some kind of super villainous fertilizer.'

'What's fertilizer?' Marv asked.

'It makes plants grow. Except this fertilizer makes the plants grow extra big and makes them more aggressive,' Pixel said.

Before Marv could respond, a loud voice rang out through the library.

'Oh, so you've figured out how my plant powder works? So what?! You're still too late to stop me or my plant kingdom!'

Marv sprinted after Violet Vine, ducking underneath fallen bookshelves and leaping over vines. He and Pixel chased her all the way into an empty classroom.

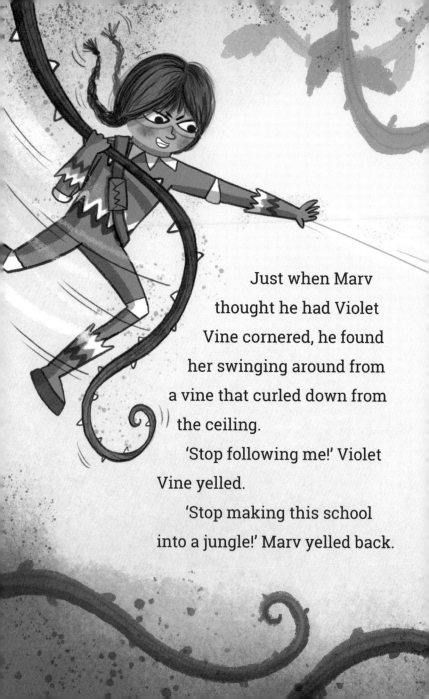

Just when Marv thought he had Violet Vine cornered, he found her swinging around from a vine that curled down from the ceiling.

'Stop following me!' Violet Vine yelled.

'Stop making this school into a jungle!' Marv yelled back.

Violet Vine thrust her wrist in Marv's direction and something shot out of the arm of her super-suit. Marv dived to one side, dodging it. A spikey thorn dart was stuck in the wall behind him.

Violet Vine began swinging out of the classroom, using more of the vines that dangled from the ceiling.

Marv ran as fast as he could, leaping over plants and dodging the thorns Violet Vine was shooting back at him.

If he wasn't being attacked, Marv
thought he'd have found this great fun. He
whooped and then somersaulted into the
air, catching a vine and matching Violet
Vine in the air, swing for swing.

A loud pinging sound beeped next to Marv. It was Pixel—the darts were pinging off her metal body. She zoomed towards Violet Vine, but just before Pixel could knock her off her vine, the supervillain struck again! Violet Vine reached into her satchel and pulled out a fistful of powder, throwing it into Pixel's face.

Pixel spun around and fell, sneezing over and over again. Marv's heart dropped.

'Pixel!' Marv jumped off his vine and went down to see if she was OK.

'Don't worry—Achoo! It's not fertilizer—Achoo! I think it's just pollen—Achoo!' Pixel said in between sneezes.

'Pollen?' Marv asked.

'Yes, I have hay fever,' Pixel said. Marv raised his eyebrows.

'I didn't know that was even possible! You're a robot!'

'Neither did I. Glad that worked though,' Violet Vine said as her vine lowered her down to meet them. 'You and your little robot friend need to recognize when you're beaten.'

'We're not beaten, we're just sneezing a little,' Pixel said defiantly.

'You know what they say, you sneeze you lose.'

'I think that's *you snooze you lose*,' Marv said. 'It's supposed to rhyme. It's not funny if it doesn't rhyme.'

'Stop attacking my jokes!' Violet Vine said with a scowl.

'Stop attacking this school!' Marv roared back.

'Maybe I will. I was going to make my plant throne in the hall but it's so tiny and poky there, and there really isn't enough light,' Violet Vine said.

'So, you're going to leave the school alone?' Marv's hopes rose for a moment.

'What?! Of course not! By now my plants should have dealt with all those pesky kids. Your school garden looks like the perfect place for me to make my throne and finally crown myself the queen of this jungle!' Violet Vine said. 'And there's nothing you can do to stop me.'

Then a giant jungle leaf swept Violet
Vine up and out of an open window,
back towards the garden.

'We need to stop her,' Marv said. He
glanced down at Pixel. 'At least you've
stopped sneezing.'

'Yep, my nose is fine now, but my eyes are still stinging. Nothing a bit of water can't fix,' Pixel said, squirting her face with jets of water that shot out from her fingertips.

Water. That gave Marv an idea.

'Pixel, let's head back out to the garden. It's time to clean this jungle up!'

CHAPTER 6

Marv raced back to the garden—he was right on Violet Vine's tail.

'Are you still chasing after me?' Vine said as she glanced behind her. 'Aren't you tired?! We've been doing this all day!'

'If you stop being a supervillain, I'll stop chasing you,' Marv yelled back.

In response, Violet Vine acted even more like a supervillain. She grabbed another handful of powder from her satchel and slammed it into the ground.

Vines poured out of the earth, blocking Marv's way.

'Super-suit, activate rocket boosters!' Marv said as fast as he could. Immediately, a pair of rocket boosters emerged from the back of his super-suit. He snatched up Pixel just as the boosters roared, powering them up into the air and over the vines.

'Argggghhhhh!' Marv yelled as he flew. His speed was almost uncontrollable.

From this high up, Marv could see the entire playground. Joe and Eva had freed all their classmates, but something wicked was heading their way. Violet Vine!

Marv whizzed down and landed as close to her as he could get, but Violet Vine saw him coming.

'You know, I need something a little bit special for my throne,' she said, tipping over her satchel and emptying all the powder inside onto the ground.

'Not good!' Pixel yelped.

'Noooo!' Marv shouted, but it was too late.

A mountain of huge plants

exploded up from the ground—
vines, ferns, thorny bushes, and
Venus flytraps—practically every
plant Marv had seen that day was
there. And it was all in the shape
of an enormous throne. Violet
Vine scrambled up the towering
mass of plants and sat on top. She
smirked, looking triumphant, but
her expression didn't last long.

The vines kept growing, getting
bigger and bigger. The shape
of the throne was getting more
misshapen with each passing
second, and that wasn't all—the
vines began to wrap themselves
around Violet Vine herself. It was

like they had a mind of their own. She couldn't control the plants any more.

'Help! Help!' Violet Vine called out.

Marv didn't hesitate.

'Super-suit, please activate water jet!' Marv said, placing his hand on the 'M' symbol of his suit.

A panel in the arm of his super-suit opened and Marv pulled out a giant Super Soaker, filled with water.

Marv blasted the plants with water from the Super Soaker. The powdery dust was washed off the plants that made up Violet Vine's throne.

The supervillain shrieked as the throne shrivelled and dried out, before it finally cracked and fell apart. Violet Vine rolled off the throne onto the ground. She was completely soaked.

'Water surprise,' Pixel said, nudging Marv. 'What a surprise. Get it?'

'I get it,' Marv replied with a grin.

As Marv stepped towards Violet, he felt a vine slithering round his ankle. Before he could shake it off, Marv was lifted high into the air and left dangling upside down.

'You'll never catch me!' Violet Vine cackled, getting up and making a run for it. Marv aimed his Super Soaker at the vine holding his ankle and it released him. He somersaulted in the air, landing gracefully, ready to chase Violet Vine.

But she had already disappeared, and Marv had a school to save.

There were still plenty of overgrown plants left across the school, so Marv ran at super speed, using the Super Soaker to destroy all the vines and other plants, while Pixel put all the tables and chairs, back in their places.

When they were finished, Marv ran back to his hiding place behind the bin, and quickly got changed as Pixel climbed into his backpack.

When Marvin ran back out into the playground he found Eva standing with Joe, holding her now soggy garden design.

'Are you OK?' Marvin asked.

'I'm fine,' Eva huffed, but Marvin could see that she wasn't OK. 'I was just so happy when I won the design competition, but now it's all for nothing and everything is ruined.'

Marvin reached out and hugged Eva. He got it now—Eva was just as passionate about her design as he had been about his. Maybe the similarities in their designs were just a coincidence. He knew Eva, and she wasn't the sort of person to cheat. He couldn't believe that he'd accused her of copying him. Eva had a great design—she didn't deserve to have it ruined by Violet Vine.

'I'm sorry for what I said earlier, Eva. You won fair and square and I was just being a sore loser,' Marvin said.

'It's OK. I know how badly you wanted to win and your hothouse idea was really cool, but I did do my own research and I would never cheat! Anyway, it's all ruined now,' Eva said, looking around at the destroyed garden.

'No, it's not! We're going to rebuild the garden and it'll be better than ever.'

'Totally,' agreed Joe, 'but maybe this time without the creepy vines and human-eating Venus flytraps!'

'Yeah, I think we've had enough of vines and Venus flytraps. I might change the part about the hothouse. Maybe you could help me redesign it, Marv?' Eva smiled.

'I'd love to,' Marvin grinned back.

ABOUT THE AUTHOR

ALEX FALASE-KOYA

Alex is a London native. He has been writing children's fiction since he was a teenager and was a winner of Spread the Word's 2019 London Writers Awards for YA and Children's. He co-wrote *The Breakfast Club Adventures*, the first fiction book by Marcus Rashford. He now lives in Walthamstow with his girlfriend and two cats.

ABOUT THE ILLUSTRATOR

PAULA BOWLES

Paula grew up in Hertfordshire, and has
always loved drawing, reading, and using
her imagination, so she studied illustration
at Falmouth College of Arts and became an
illustrator. She now lives in Bristol, and has
worked as an illustrator for over ten years, and
has had books published with Nosy Crow and
Simon & Schuster.

MARV

Marvin's life changed when he found an old superhero suit and became MARV. The suit has been passed down through Marvin's family and was last worn by his grandad. It's powered by the kindness and imagination of the wearer and doesn't work for just anybody.

COURAGE	7
FRIENDSHIP	9
KINDNESS	9
POWERS	10
AGILITY	7
COMBAT SKILLS	6

PIXEL

PIXEL is Marv's brave superhero sidekick. Her quick thinking and unwavering loyalty make her the perfect crime-fighting companion.

COURAGE	6
FRIENDSHIP	10
KINDNESS	9
POWERS	5
AGILITY	7
COMBAT SKILLS	5

VIOLET VINE

Violet Vine is a villain with a special interest in plants. She has no natural superpowers but uses her scientific knowledge to create powders and potions that turn ordinary plants deadly.

COURAGE	8
FRIENDSHIP	2
KINDNESS	4
POWERS	4
AGILITY	6
COMBAT SKILLS	6

'THE SUPER-SUIT IS POWERED BY TWO THINGS: **KINDNESS** AND **IMAGINATION**. LUCKILY YOU, MARVIN, HAVE TONS OF BOTH!'

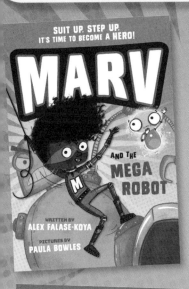

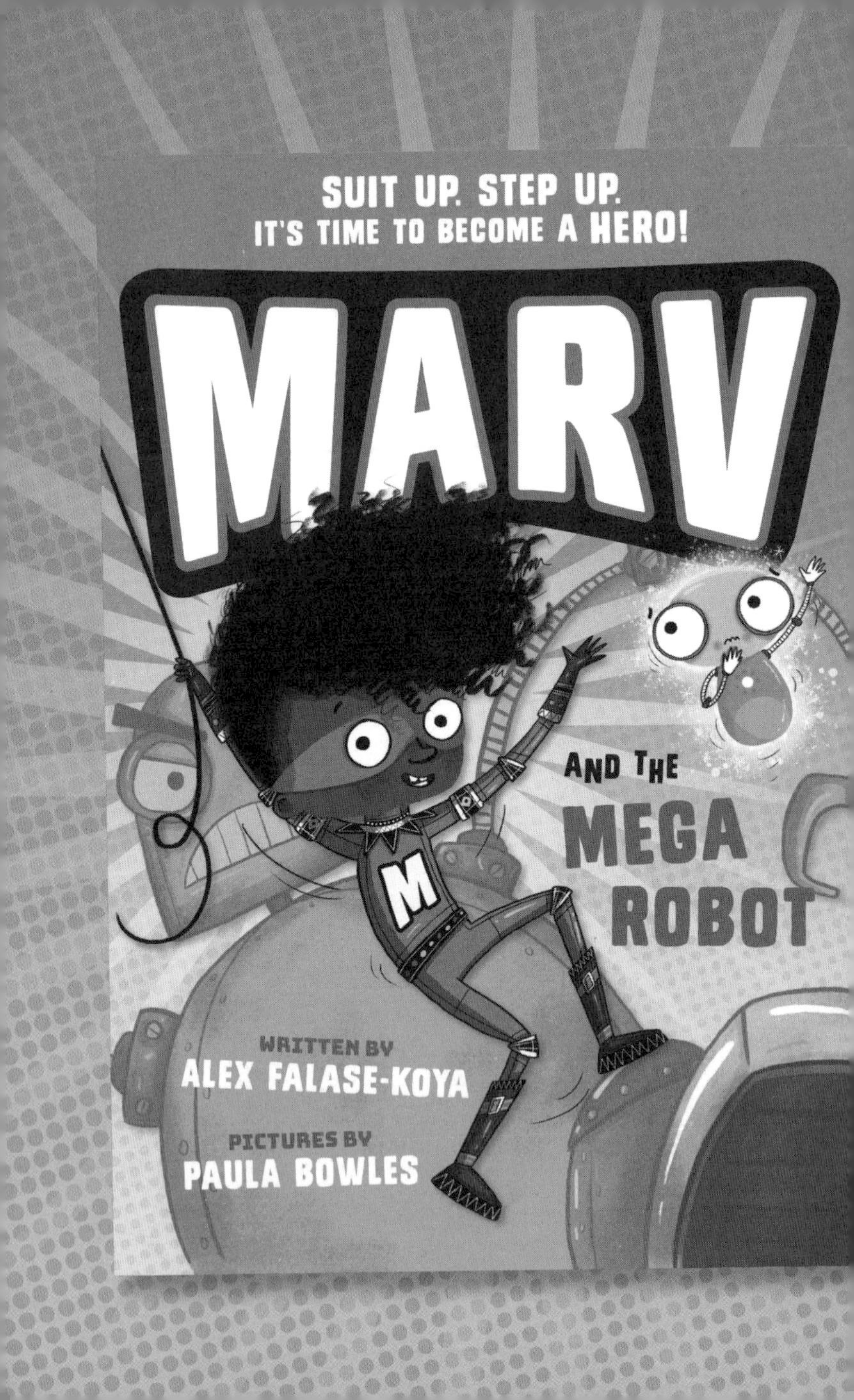
SUIT UP. STEP UP.
IT'S TIME TO BECOME A HERO!
MARV
AND THE
MEGA
ROBOT
WRITTEN BY
ALEX FALASE-KOYA
PICTURES BY
PAULA BOWLES
M

'THE SUPER-SUIT IS POWERED BY TWO THINGS: KINDNESS AND IMAGINATION. LUCKILY YOU, MARVIN, HAVE TONS OF BOTH!'

Marvin loves reading about superheroes and now he's about to become one for real.

Grandad is passing his superhero suit and robot sidekick, Pixel, on to Marvin. It's been a long time since the world needed a superhero but now, with a mega robot and a supervillain on the loose, that time has come.

To defeat his enemies and protect his friends, Marvin must learn to trust the superhero within. Only then will Marvin become MARV – unstoppable, invincible, and **totally marvellous!**

LOVE MARV?
WHY NOT TRY THESE TOO...?

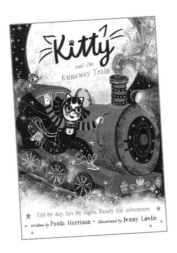